Carmen Learns English

by **Judy Cox**

illustrated by
Angela Dominguez

Holiday House
New York

The publisher would like to thank Lena Burgos-Lafuente of New York University's Department of Spanish and Portuguese for reviewing the Spanish in this book for accuracy.

Text copyright © 2010 by Judy Cox
Illustrations copyright © 2010 by Angela Dominguez
All Rights Reserved
HOLIDAY HOUSE is registered in the U.S. Patent and Trademark Office.
Printed and Bound in May 2010 at Kwong Fat Offset Printing Co., Ltd., Dongguan City, Quangdong Province, China.
The text typeface is Providence Sans.
The artwork was created with ink, watercolors, and acrylics on Strathmore illustration board.
www.holidayhouse.com
First Edition
1 3 5 7 9 10 8 6 4 2

Library of Congress Cataloging-in-Publication Data
Cox, Judy.
Carmen learns English / by Judy Cox ; illustrated by Angela N. Dominguez. — 1st ed.
p. cm.
Summary: Newly-arrived in the United States from Mexico,
Carmen is apprehensive about going to school and learning English.
ISBN 978-0-8234-2174-9 (hardcover)
[1. English language—Fiction. 2. Mexican Americans—Fiction.
3. Schools—Fiction. 4. Immigrants—Fiction.]
I. Dominguez, Angela N., ill. II. Title.
PZ7.C83835Car 2010
[E]—dc22
2008048462

To all my English Language Learners
—J. C.

To mi hermano, Mom, Dad, Jessica, and
the nephew or niece on the way
—A. D.

Next fall my little sister, Lupita, starts school. And I want her to speak English good like I do. So I told her, listen to me.

The first day of school was scary. Mami gave me a hug and said, "Be brave, Carmen, *mi hijita.*" Then she kissed me good-bye.

I sat at my desk in the classroom with a sad heart. I wanted to go home, but I had to stay at school and be brave.

So many kids! And no one spoke Spanish. They talked *muy* fast and I did not understand. I put my head down on my desk and my tears came out.

"*Hola,*" I heard someone say. I raised my head. It was a tall lady with yellow hair and a silver whistle around her neck. She smiled at me. "*Mi nombre es Señora Coski,*" she said. "*Soy su maestra.*"

My teacher! Her Spanish sounded *muy* terrible! And I could see that she would not laugh at me if my English was terrible too.

Later that day, I had to be very brave. I didn't know where the bathroom was. "¿*Dónde está el baño, por favor?*" I asked. The *niños* who sat at my table shook their heads because they did not understand. Just in time, la Señora Coski showed everyone *el baño*.

"Restroom,'" she told me.

I nodded. In my head, I repeated the word over and over so I would not forget. "¿Dónde está el restroom?" I whispered.

When I got home, I taught Lupita that important new word.

The next day, we sang a song about a yellow bus. "Chellow bus," I repeated to myself. I liked the sound of the words, but I did not know what they meant until it was time to go home.

La Señora Coski pointed to the school bus. "Yellow bus," she told me.

"¡Amarillo!" I shouted. "¡Camión escolar! Yellow bus! Yellow! Yellow!"

When I got home, I drew an amarillo bus for Lupita. We hung it on the wall over her bed.

All week, la Señora Coski sang the colors. She pointed them out on a rainbow chart that hung above the board.

At home I drew rainbows for Lupita and Mami and I told them the colors in English—yellow, blue, red, green, orange, pur-ple (that was a hard one).

But I still was not brave enough to say them at school.

The next week, la Señora Coski sang
the ABC song. All the kids joined in.
"Sing it with us," said la Señora Coski.
I was too shy. But at home Lupita and
I held hands and skipped around the
fig tree singing, "A, B, C, D. . ."
In school I learned about Jack
and Jill and the pail and the hill,
and Humpty Dumpty and all
the king's men. At home
I taught the rhymes
to Lupita while we
played a game I
had learned at
recess: hopscotch.

During recess, Mikki taught me jump rope rhymes, and we skipped rope across the playground, chanting, "Texaco, Texaco, all the way from Mexico. . ."

When it was time to line up, la Señora Coski blew her silver whistle. It made a very loud noise. All the *niños* ran to line up. I grinned at Mikki. I wanted a whistle like that so everyone would listen to me!

One day, la Señora Coski wrote the numbers on the number line. I was happy to see those numbers. I knew them all!

"Uno, dos, tres, cuatro, cinco, seis," I shouted in Spanish.

"Mrs. Coski!" said Mikki. "Carmen didn't say them right!"

I put my hands on my hips and made a mad face at her. *I do say them right,* I wanted to say. *I say them in Spanish!* But I didn't have the English words to tell her so.

La Señora Coski smiled at me. "Let's all count in Spanish," she said. "Carmen can learn English, and we can learn Spanish."

"Okay," I said. I felt brave again—I was teaching them Spanish!

From then on I had to be the teacher two times every day. At home I taught Lupita English, and at school I taught la Señora Coski and the kids to speak Spanish.

I learned to say "please" instead of "por favor," and my class learned to say "gracias" for "thank you." Every morning I came to school and said, "Good morning," and the kids said, "¡Buenos días!"; and when I got on the bus to go home, I said, "Good-bye, Señora Coski," and she said, "¡Adiós, amiga!"

But school was not all the time good. Because sometimes on the playground I heard bad things. One day, I heard a big boy tell his *amigo* that I talk funny. "You got a funny accent," the boy said to me.

For a moment I wished I was back in Mexico, where all the people speak Spanish and no one makes fun of me.

But then I was angry, and it made me brave. I put my hands on my hips the way Mami does when something does not please her.

"Excuse me?" I said as polite as la Señora Coski. "Excuse me? I don't got an accent. It's you who got the accent!"

Those big boys stared at me with their mouths hanging open like they were catching flies, and I laughed to see them so.

I walked over to the swings and Mikki said, "¡Hola, Carmen! Will you swing with me, ¿por favor?"

"Yes," I said. "Let's swing." I pumped my legs hard and that swing flew above the playground and I saw all the kids running and jumping and playing and la Señora Coski watching them. Her silver whistle shone in the sun.

And I think to myself, How much I have learned.

Next fall, Lupita starts school. And she will say to her teacher, "Good morning. My name is Lupita and I am in kindergarten!"

I think I will be a teacher when I grow up and wear a silver whistle around my neck.

Like Mrs. Coski.

GLOSSARY

Adiós, amiga.—Good-bye, girl
friend.

amarillo—yellow

amigo—pal

buenos días—good morning

camión escolar—school bus

¿Dónde está el baño?—Where is
the bathroom?

gracias—thank you

hola— hi

mi hijita—my little daughter

Mi nombre es Señora Coski.—My
name is Mrs. Coski.

muy—very

niños—children

por favor—please

Soy tu maestra.—I am your teacher.

uno, dos, tres, cuatro, cinco, seis—
one, two, three, four, five, six